BIG SHOT

With thanks to Emma, who is my Big Shot.

First published 2012 by A & C Black,
an imprint of Bloomsbury Publishing Plc
50 Bedford Square, London WC1B 3DP

www.acblack.com
www.bloomsbury.com

Copyright © 2012 A & C Black
Text copyright © 2012 Sean Callery
Illustration copyright © 2012 Jamie Lenman

The rights of Sean Callery and Jamie Lenman to be identified
as the author and illustrator of this work respectively, have been asserted by
them in accordance with the Copyrights, Designs and Patents Act 1988.

ISBN 978-1-4081-7409-8

This book is produced using paper that is made from wood
grown in managed, sustainable forests. It is natural, renewable
and recyclable. The logging and manufacturing processes conform
to the environmental regulations of the country of origin.

Printed by CPI Group (UK), Croydon, CR0 4YY

1 3 5 7 9 10 8 6 4 2

recommended by
www.catchup.org

Catch Up is a not-for-profit charity
which aims to address the problem of
underachievement that has its roots in
literacy and numeracy difficulties.

BIG SHOT

SEAN CALLERY

A & C Black • London

Contents

Chapter 1

Piggy

Ash watched the cricket ball falling from the sky. This was it. He was going to make a great catch.

If he caught it Mr Naylor would put him in the team. He would finally be one of the big shots at school.

"Stay back, Danny," he said to his friend. "This ball is mine."

WHACK! The ball smashed into Ash's
face. His nose felt as if it had blown up.

Danny dived to catch the ball. He
grabbed it and threw it like a rocket. It was
a great throw. The ball knocked down the
cricket stumps.

"Wow," said the wicket keeper.

"Come here, Danny," called Mr Naylor. He picked up the team sheet.

As Danny walked towards Mr Naylor, he heard Grant hiss, "Welcome to the team, Piggy!" Grant was the captain of the team. Danny's face went as red as the cricket ball. He turned and ran towards the changing rooms.

* * *

Danny was the new boy at school. He had moved in next door to Ash a few weeks ago. They made friends walking to school. Danny was a tall, strong boy, but he was quiet and shy in class. He was always eating. So Grant called him 'Piggy'.

Ash never joined in with the pig noises that Grant and the other kids made. Once Ash had told them to stop but they just laughed. Ash was scared they might pick on him too.

"What's up with your mate?" Grant asked Ash as Danny ran off the cricket pitch.

"He doesn't like it when you call him names," said Ash.

"He should lay off the chips then," laughed Grant.

Mr Naylor came over and looked at Ash's nose. "Nothing broken. Go and see what's up with Danny. And no messing about," he told Ash.

Chapter 2

Tango

Danny ran all the way to the changing room. It was empty. He started to do a slow dance around the room. Dancing always made him feel better.

When Ash came in he was amazed to see
Danny dancing.

"What are you doing?" asked Ash.

"Promise you won't tell?" Danny said.
"My big sister makes me go with her to
ballroom dance classes."

"I felt silly doing it at first," Danny went on. "The music is rubbish and you have to wear stupid clothes. But I'm good at it."

"What dances do you do?" asked Ash.

"All sorts. Like this," said Danny. He took a step sideways and spun round fast.

"Cool," laughed Ash. "Teach me!"

Danny did it again. Ash had a try but his feet didn't do what he wanted. He slipped on the shiny floor and grabbed at Danny.

The two boys fell through the changing room door just as the rest of the players arrived.

"What are you two doing?" shouted Mr Naylor.

Then Ash made a big mistake. "Danny was teaching me the tango, sir," he said.

Danny froze. The players all laughed. Some of them made pig noises. Mr Naylor glared at Ash and Danny. "I warned you not to mess about," he said.

Ash thought things couldn't get worse. He was wrong.

Chapter 3

Litter Pick

Just then Miss Hopper, the PE teacher, came over.

"Can I have a word with this lot, Mr Naylor?" she said.

"Go ahead," he huffed.

"The county sports trials are on Friday. There are some places to fill," said Miss Hopper. "I'll be running extra sports clubs every lunchtime."

Ash wanted to show his friend he was sorry.

"Shall we do that, Danny?" Ash asked.

Someone made a pig noise. Danny went red. He shoved Ash away.

"Right, that's it," said Mr Naylor. "I'm fed up with you two causing trouble. You can do a litter pick every lunchtime for a week."

The litter pick was worse than being kept back after lessons. The whole school saw you filling bags with rubbish. Danny glared at Ash, and ran off.

Chapter 4

Phone Picture

Ash's hand shook as he knocked on
Mr Naylor's door. Would his plan work?
"Come in," said Mr Naylor.

"Sir, Danny and I want to go to Miss Hopper's sports club," he said.

Mr Naylor looked up. "Really?"

"Yes sir, but we can't go if we have to pick up litter."

The wall clock ticked ten times. It felt like the longest ten seconds of Ash's life.

"OK," said Mr Naylor. "But if I see any more messing about, you'll be picking up litter for a month."

* * *

Ash told Danny what he had done but his friend didn't even look at him. Ash was pleased when Danny showed up on the sports field at lunchtime.

"OK, then, Ash. Let's try the long jump," said Miss Hopper. "You should be good at it with your long legs."

Ash found he always started with his right foot. He liked counting out his steps before making his jump.

"Not bad," said Miss Hopper. "But stop swinging your arms like a gorilla."

"Beats doing a litter pick, doesn't it?"
Ash said to Danny.

"Look at this," said Danny. He pulled
out his phone and showed Ash a picture
from a website someone had sent him.

Ash's face was pasted on the head of a woman in a pink ballroom dancing dress. Next to this was Danny's face stuck on the body of a pig.

"You and your big mouth," hissed Danny.

"No phones in school," said Miss Hopper. She took the phone and put it in her bag.

"Shall we carry on?" she said.

Danny stared at the ground as he followed Miss Hopper away.

Chapter 5

Banned

The next day a gang of boys was waiting for them at the school gates.

"Where's your dress?" someone called to Ash.

The gang started making pig noises as Danny walked past.

Miss Hopper came over and told them to stop.

Then she said to Danny and Ash, "Make sure you come to sports club at lunchtime. You did really well yesterday."

That lunchtime they tried the triple jump. Danny was too slow. Ash was fast on the runway and could power through the hop, skip and jump.

"Not bad," said Miss Hopper. "Grant jumped longer than you, but you can be the sub at the sports trials on Friday."

Miss Hopper turned to Danny. She said, "You're strong and you've got good balance. I want to enter you in a throwing event like the discus."

She took Danny to the throwing circle. "Start by facing away from where you will throw it, and bend your knees." She told him how to swing his body then spin round and throw the discus.

"May I have a word please, Miss Hopper?" It was Mr Naylor. Miss Hopper hurried over to talk to him.

"Go on, Danny," said Ash. Danny spun round and threw the discus. It zoomed high across the field and into some bushes.

"Wow, great throw," said Ash.

Danny smiled for the first time in ages
and the two boys raced to find the discus.
Ash tried a couple of dance moves across
the grass. Danny laughed and showed him
how to do them. Then they grabbed some
branches to smash into the bushes and hunt
for the discus.

But Mr Naylor was right behind them.

"You two messing about again," he said.

"Come to me tomorrow to get the rubbish

bags. You're banned from the sports trials."

Chapter 6

Escape

Next morning, Ash and Danny passed
the school minibus as they went into school.

"Is everybody here? We're a bit late,"
called out Miss Hopper.

She threw the big kit bag into the back of the minibus and closed the doors. Then she rushed round to the driver's seat and started the engine.

Ash saw the gang of kids who had been nasty the day before waiting in the playground.

"It's not fair that we're banned from the sports trials," Ash said.

"True," said Danny.

"And I'm fed up with that lot," said Ash, looking at the gang in the playground.

Ash opened the back door of the minibus. He shoved Danny onto the floor and closed the door behind them.

"What are you doing?" whispered Danny, as the bus rumbled away from school.

"We're going to the sports trials," said Ash. "I'm sure Miss Hopper will understand."

*   *   *

The minibus stopped. Grant came round to open the back doors. When he pulled out the kit bag he saw Ash and Danny. He leapt back in surprise and tripped over.

"Ow, my foot!" he cried.

"What's up?" called Miss Hopper as she rushed round. "What are you two doing here?" she said, staring at Ash and Danny.

"Please Miss, we wanted to come," said Ash.

Grant groaned. "My ankle. It really hurts."

Miss Hopper checked his foot. "It's twisted. Now we're a man down, thanks to you two." She phoned the school to say the two boys were with her.

"It's too late to take you back," she hissed. "Sit with Grant. Don't do *anything*."

Chapter 7

Triple Jump

Danny stared across the track.

Grant stared at his foot. It was swollen and painful.

Ash stared at the scoreboard. "Look, we're only a few points off the top score," he said.

"If I did the triple jump we'd get some points," said Grant. "But I can't even stand on this ankle."

Ash jumped up. "Give me your bib."

"Why?" said Grant.

"I can do the triple jump," said Ash.

"Miss Hopper told you to stay here," said Danny.

"Come on, give it to me," said Ash.

"Go on then," said Grant. "But Mr Naylor is going to go *nuts*."

Ash knew Grant was right, but he wanted to prove he was good at something.

He put on the bib, gave his details to the scorer and marked out his start point. He set off down the runway.

Thump. He took off on his right foot and rose up.

Thump. He landed on the same foot and pushed on.

Thump. He jumped off from his left foot. It felt like flying. Sand hurt his eyes as he landed.

"Good jump, lad. Work on that landing," said a man as he wrote the score down.

"Nice one, Ash," shouted Grant.

Miss Hopper ran up. "I told you to stay with Grant," she snapped.

"You've got a bit of a star here," said the man. "He's just come second in the triple jump."

"That's twenty points, Miss – it puts us into second place," said Danny quickly.

"Well, that's good," said Miss Hopper. "But there's only one event to go and we aren't in it. We can't win."

Chapter 8

Big Shot

Ash turned away and nearly fell over a
shiny ball lying on the grass. Feeling angry,
he kicked the ball. It felt like kicking a brick.

The ball hardly moved. "Ow!" he cried.

"Serves you right," said Miss Hopper.

"That's a shot put. It's the ball for the last event."

The man with the score sheet picked up
the metal ball and gave it to a boy nearby.
"Right, lad," he said, "I want to see those
feet dancing."

"What does he mean about feet
dancing?" asked Ash.

"Shot put isn't that different from
throwing the discus," said Miss Hopper.
"You sort of dance across and throw the ball
from inside a little circle."

"Danny could do that. He's got dancing feet," said Ash.

Miss Hopper looked at Danny. "How about it, Danny?" she asked.

"Go on," said Ash. "You're brilliant at throwing."

"OK," said Danny.

Miss Hopper gave him some advice. "Push the ball into your neck and point your elbow," she said. "Try to glide across the throwing circle."

Danny studied the other throwers. He was used to watching and copying people in his dance classes. The moves were like a dance. He could do this.

"You're next," said the man with the clip board.

Danny's hands felt sweaty. He moved across the circle but the shot put slipped as he threw it. The ball went high but didn't go far.

"Wait. Wipe your hands," said Miss Hopper. She gave Danny a towel and turned to the scorer. "He gets a second throw, doesn't he? Come on Danny, do it like a dance."

This time Danny glided across the circle and threw the shot put in one easy move. The metal ball landed with a thud, way past the pegs that marked the other throws.

"Wow!" said the man. "That makes your school the winning team."

Miss Hopper phoned the school while the happy team got back into the minibus. They sang about being winners all the way back. Miss Hopper was the loudest.

Back at school, Mr Naylor came up. "I should make you pick up litter for the rest of this term," he told Ash and Danny, "but Miss Hopper says you were brilliant at the trials. Do the litter pick for the rest of this week and we'll leave it at that."

Ash and Danny picked up the litter bags. Grant took one too and limped as fast as he could to catch them up.

"Hold on, Big Shot," said Grant to Danny. "It'll be quicker with three of us."

Attack of
the Killer Frogs

Lily saw the giant frogs in the garden. Mum
and Dad don't believe her. But Lily knows
the frogs are coming to get her. Soon. Maybe
even tonight... Can Lily escape the attack
of the killer frogs?

ISBN 978-1-4081-5268-3
RRP £5.99

Rainbow Boots

All the cool kids have Rainbow Boots. All except Denzil. So he tells a lie about the special pair he's going to get… Soon the lies are piling up. Can Denzil find a way out of his web of lies?

ISBN 978-1-4081-7408-1
RRP £5.99

Shadow Snatcher

When Eva was a baby, Death stole her
shadow. It was just a matter of time before
he came back to claim Eva's life too. Can
Aiden come up with a plan to save his little
sister? Or will Death have the last laugh?

ISBN 978-1-4081-5485-4
RRP £5.99

Looking for a longer read?

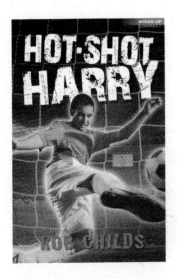

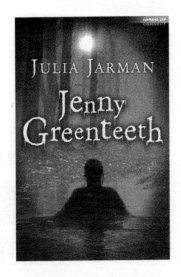